THE ADVENTURES OF Hemo

By: Kimberly R. L. Booker

DEDICATION:

To my husband, William, daughter, Allison and son, Jaelin who were the inspiration for The Adventures of Hemo book series.

ACKNOWLEDGMENTS:

To my family who were the inspiration for this book, William, Allison and Jaelin; you guys rock my world and I am indebted to you as you each were utterly beneficial and played a critical role in the early developmental and illustrative stages of The Adventures of Hemo book series. I am humble, grateful and so thankful to have such great love and support; thanks for believing in me from the very beginning! Thanks, to my mom, Christine M. Lester, whose love for reading did not go unnoticed and also my father, Benjamin F. Lester, whose nickname was Hemo and inspired the character's name for the book. To my nana, Alene H. Clinton, for always being there and loving me unconditionally; you nurtured me in ways that I continue to constantly draw strength from; I will forever feel your presence. To my brothers and sister, uncles, aunts, nieces, nephews and cousins whom I love dearly; To Al Stafford, who was like a grandfather to me; your shared wisdom continues to flow and resonate. To the Hemo Team of Miriam Glover, my editor, and Alexander Watkins, my illustrator: you each listened, heard, and understood both the vision and mission of The Adventures of Hemo series. You saw it with passion, clarity, and love and greatly assisted me to bring the first book of The Adventures of Hemo series to life, just how I imagined it. You each allowed me the space and room to be extremely creative and tendered professional courtesy and wisdom during this process. To my friends who truly know me, warts and all, but love me anyway; To everyone, young and old that see themselves in this book; A very special shout out to my hometown folks who while growing up as children in Springfield, Massachusetts, visited their local library especially the Winchester Square Library, now known as the Mason Square Library... holla! Finally, most importantly and above all else, I thank you God, for surrounding me with your everlasting love, guidance and protection.

THE ADVENTURES OF HEMO

Copyright © *2019 by* **Kimberly R. L. Booker**

The Adventures of Hemo

ISBN: 9781085813150

1. African American Family   2. Family   3. Black love

Library of Congress Registration Number: TXu 1-888-618

Published in Dallas, Texas

Please send your comments and requests for information to Kimberly Booker via email at: Kimberly@theadventuresofhemo.com

Book editor: Miriam Glover Marketing
Graphic designs: Aestheticz Inc.

For more information about speaking engagements or to order multiple copies, please contact us at: Kimberly@theadventuresofhemo.com

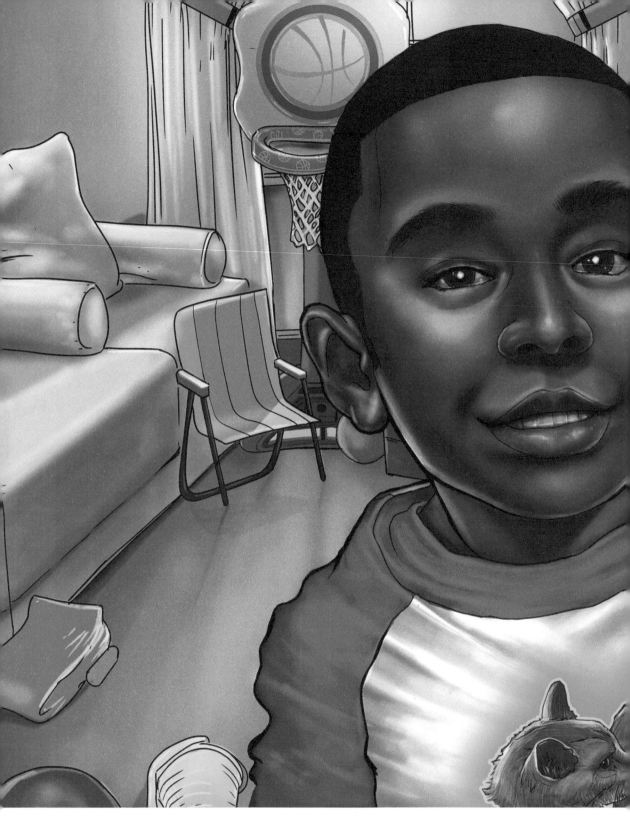

Hi, my name is Hemo and I am 3 years old. I'm proud of my name.

I was named after my Grampa. It was his
nickname way before I was born!

My two best friends are my cat named Spaz and my dog named Lexi. We have so much fun together.

When I teach them new tricks, my mommy and daddy let me give them their favorite treats. Do you have any pets?

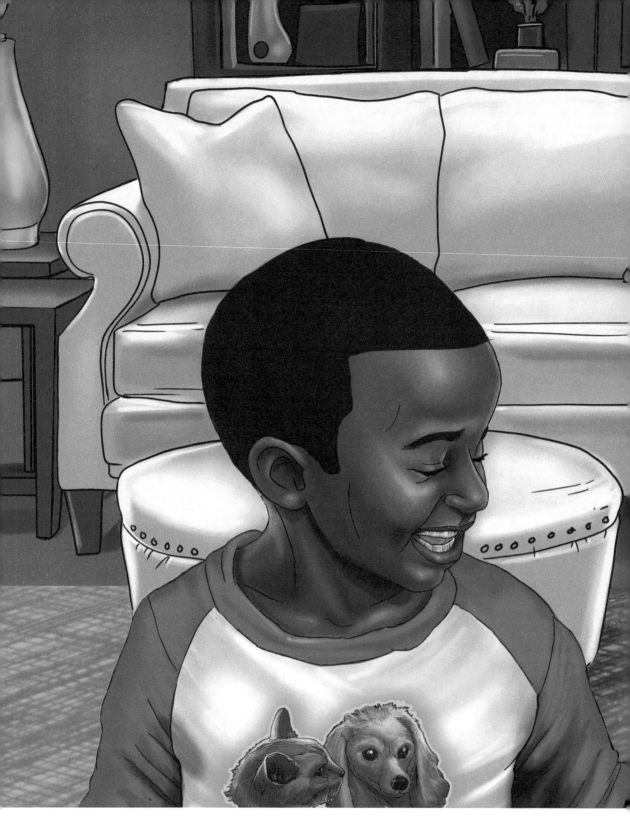

I like hanging out with my mommy. She is so funny and makes me laugh a lot.

She tells the best knock-knock jokes ever!
Who is someone that makes you laugh?

My favorite toys aren't toys at all. I really enjoy playing with the pots and pans in the kitchen next to mommy.

Sometimes, I pretend I am a famous chef! What do you like to pretend to do?

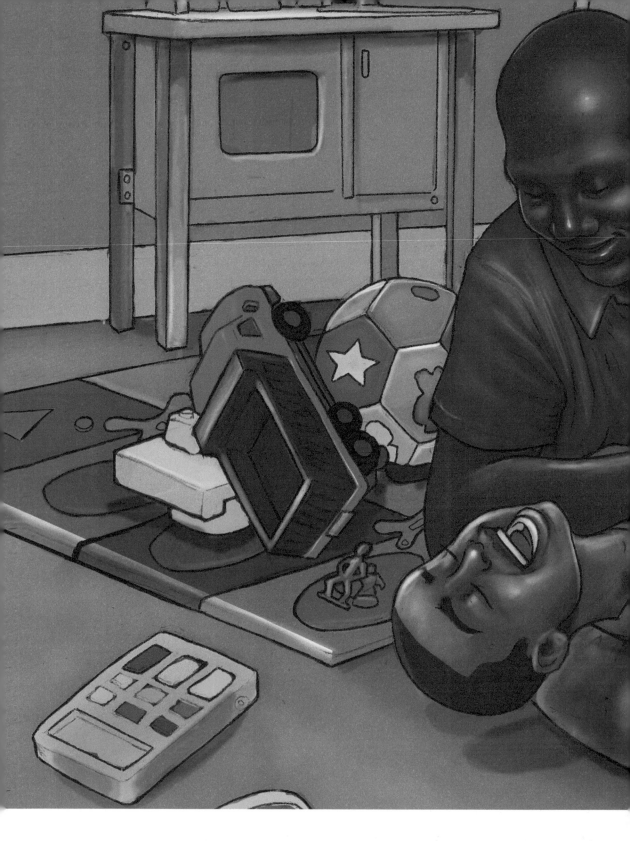

The best part of my day is tickle time with my daddy.

What's the best part of your day?

My daddy is my superhero and I am his sidekick. He has big muscles and is super strong too!

He can carry me, Spaz, and Lexi all at the same time! Together, we can do anything!

Meet my sister, Lee-lee. She is teaching me how to use the computer.

I am getting really good at it too! What are you good at?

I love my family

and my family loves me.

Post Reading Activity Quiz

What is the main character's name?

How old is Hemo?

What family member was Hemo named after?

What are the names of Hemo's pets?

Who makes Hemo laugh a lot?

What are Hemo's favorite toys?

Who does he pretend to be while playing with his favorite toys?

Who can carry Lexi, Spaz, and Hemo all at the same time?

Who is teaching Hemo how to use the computer?

Who loves Hemo very much?

ANWERS: Hemo, 3 Years Old, His Grampa, Lexi and Spaz, His Mommy, Pots and Pans, A Chef, His Daddy, His Sister Lee-lee, His Family